MX

CHAMPIONS

The stars of the show–past and present

Stephen Timblin

CRABTREE PUBLISHING COMPANY
www.crabtreebooks.com

Crabtree Publishing Company

www.crabtreebooks.com

Coordinating editor: Chester Fisher
Series and project editor: Shoreline Publishing Group LLC
Author: Stephen Timblin
Series Consultant: Bryan Stealey
Project Manager: Kavita Lad
Art direction: Rahul Dhiman
Design: Tarang Saggar
Cover Design: Ranjan Singh
Photo research: Akansha Srivastava
Editors: Adrianna Morganelli, Mike Hodge

Acknowledgments

p4: Terry Good Collections; p5: Joël Robert archive/Terry Good Collections (top); p5: ASSOCIATED PRESS (bottom); p6: Simon Cudby; p7: Paul Buckley; p8: Simon Cudby (all); p9: Simon Cudby (all); p10: Randy Petree; p11: Simon Cudby; p12: Simon Cudby; p13: Simon Cudby (all); p14: Simon Cudby; p15: Simon Cudby; p16: Simon Cudby; p17: Simon Cudby; p18: Simon Cudby; p19: Simon Cudby (all); p20: Simon Cudby; p21: Simon Cudby (all); p22: Simon Cudby (all); p23: Simon Cudby (all); p24: Simon Cudby; p25: Simon Cudby (all); p26: Simon Cudby; p27: Paul Buckley; p28: Matt Ware; p29: Simon Cudby (top); p29: Ashley Fiolek Archive (bottom); p30: Simon Cudby; p31: Simon Cudby (all)

Cover and title page image provided by Jeff Gross/Getty Images

Library and Archives Canada Cataloguing in Publication

Tamblin, Stephan
MX champions / Stephan Tamblin.

(MXplosion!)
Includes index.
ISBN 978-0-7787-3989-0 (bound).--ISBN 978-0-7787-4002-5 (pbk.)

1. Motorcyclists--Biography--Juvenile literature. 2. Motocross--Juvenile literature. I. Title. II. Series.

GV1060.2.A1T34 2008 j796.7'560922 C2008-901717-X

Library of Congress Cataloging-in-Publication Data

Library of Congress Cataloging-in-Publication Data

Tamblin, Stephen.
MX champions / Stephen Tamblin.
p. cm. -- (MXplosion!)
Includes index.
ISBN-13: 978-0-7787-4002-5 (pbk. : alk. paper)
ISBN-10: 0-7787-4002-1 (pbk. : alk. paper)
ISBN-13: 978-0-7787-3989-0 (reinforced library binding : alk. paper)
ISBN-10: 0-7787-3989-9 (reinforced library binding : alk. paper)
1. Motorcyclists--Biography--Juvenile literature. 2. Motocross--Juvenile literature. I. Title.
GV1060.2.A1T36 2008
796.7'560922--dc22
[B]

2008010873

Crabtree Publishing Company

www.crabtreebooks.com 1-800-387-7650

Copyright © **2008 CRABTREE PUBLISHING COMPANY**. All rights reserved. No part of this publication may be reproduced, stored in a retrieval system or be transmitted in any form or by any means, electronic, mechanical, photocopying, recording, or otherwise, without the prior written permission of Crabtree Publishing Company. In Canada: We acknowledge the financial support of the Government of Canada through the Book Publishing Industry Development Program (BPIDP) for our publishing activities.

Published in Canada
Crabtree Publishing
616 Welland Ave.
St. Catharines, ON
L2M 5V6

Published in the United States
Crabtree Publishing
PMB16A
350 Fifth Ave., Suite 3308
New York, NY 10118

Published in the United Kingdom
Crabtree Publishing
White Cross Mills
High Town, Lancaster
LA1 4XS

Published in Australia
Crabtree Publishing
386 Mt. Alexander Rd.
Ascot Vale (Melbourne)
VIC 3032

Contents

Pioneering Heroes	4
The Championships	6
Wild Styles	8
The Man	10
It's Showtime!	12
Stefan the Great	14
G.O.A.T.	16
King James	20
The Globetrotters	22
The Triple Threat	24
The Freestyle Fellowship	26
Wonder Women	28
Villopoto Action	30
Glossary and Index	32

Pioneering Heroes

Today's motocross (MX) champions travel the globe making a great living doing what they love. They appear airborne on their bikes on the covers of magazines and books, film their own daredevil DVDs, and even star in popular video games. Before meeting today's stars, however, let's meet the sport's early champions.

Super Scrambles

Motocross started in England, when races known as **scrambles** were held throughout the countryside. When exactly the sport started, however, is still up for argument. Some date the birth of motocross back to 1914, when the manufacturing company Scott organized a race for employees in Yorkshire. Others think that the first race was between policemen and local motorcycle enthusiasts a few years later, while still more claim that the first motocross race was held in 1924, when the Southern Scott Scramble was held in England. The winner of that race, Arthur Sparks, rode a 486cc Scott Squirrel Solo. It's not known what Mr. Sparks won, but you can bet that it was nothing close to the huge checks that are cashed by today's champions.

A European Sensation

It didn't take long for the sport to cross over into mainland Europe, and by the late 1920s, motorcyclists in France, Belgium, and the Netherlands were organizing their own races. "Scrambles" wasn't an easy word to say in their native languages, so the term motocross—a combination of the French word for motorcycle (*motocylette*) and cross-country—was born.

Motocross continued to work its way across Europe, and by the 1940s, riders as far off as Sweden, Italy, and Russia were bitten by the motorbike bug. In 1947, the first motocross championship—the Motocross of Nations—was held in Holland, signaling that motocross had arrived as an official sport.

Jeff Smith shows his stuff. He was one of the top riders to emerge from England, the home of motocross riding.

Coming to America

Motocross finally began picking up fans in the United States in the 1960s. The reason? Crews of European riders started coming over to give demonstrations of their off-road skills. Once American riders witnessed high-flying greats like England's Jeff Smith and Belgium's Joël Robert in action, they wanted in on the fun. And when *On Any Sunday*, a film showcasing motocross stars, came out in 1971, motocross fever began sweeping the country. When the first major **supercross** race, called the "Super Bowl of Motocross," was held inside the Los Angeles Coliseum in 1972, photos of American riders like Marty Smith began appearing on the bedroom walls of young racing fans across the country.

American rider Marty Smith was one of the first "Yanks" to achieve success in MX not long after it arrived in the U.S. in the 1960s.

Belgium's Joël Robert (right) accepts one of his many trophies. The talented rider won six world titles.

The Championships

Who's number one? Fans and riders want to know. Two major groups run the world's biggest seasons of motocross competitions and crown new champions each year. There are also many one-day events, along with popular contests for younger amateur **riders.**

Let's get it started! MX riders begin behind a gate. When the gate drops, the dirt starts flying!

Fédération Internationale de Motocyclisme

Known simply as FIM, the Fédération Internationale de Motocyclisme was founded in Paris, France, more than 100 years ago. Since organizing the first Motocross of Nations in 1947, FIM has been in charge of the world's most important motocross races. FIM's Grand Prix World Championships feature MX1, MX2, and MX3 class races mainly in Europe, but includes what are known as "flyaways" in countries as far away as Japan and Australia. Why "flyaway"? Most riders come from Europe and America, and have to "fly away" to reach the events!

American Motorcyclist Association

Founded in 1924, the American Motorcyclist Association (AMA) is a **federation** that oversees nearly 100 professional motorcycle races within the United States each year. The organization holds both the AMA Motocross Championship and the AMA Supercross Championship, both of which have two different divisions that are based on the size of the bikes that are used in the races.

The X Games

The biggest showcase for motocross over the past decade has been the X Games, which started in 1996. These popular events have helped make stars out of riders such as Jeremy McGrath and Travis Pastrana. Organized by ESPN, the X Games have made **freestyle motocross** (FMX) a main event. The best riders in FMX now show up each year to unveil never-before-seen tricks.

One for the Rest of Us

If you hope to make it big in motocross, Loretta Lynn's ranch in Hurricane Mills, Tennessee, is the place to be. That's because the AMA Amateur National Championships are held there every summer. The world's biggest and most important amateur motocross event attracts more than 20,000 amateur hopefuls who are attempting to earn a spot in the week-long competition. Past winners include the finest champions in modern motocross history, including Ricky Carmichael, Travis Pastrana, and James Stewart.

Riders in the X Games perform amazing freestyle aerial *tricks before packed arenas.*

Wild Styles

The popularity of motocross and the thrill-seeking nature of its riders have combined to create many different riding styles. The following are the most popular, and each has created its own share of champions.

Motocross

Motocross races are held outdoors on mainly natural off-road courses. Often shortened to "MX" or even "MotoX," these races take place on tracks that are made of dirt, mud, grass, and sand. These courses can be as long as two grueling miles (3.2 km). Courses vary in style greatly—sometimes they might not even have jumps—but most motocross races feature 40 riders blasting through a course at the same time. In the U.S., races are divided into Motocross and Motocross Lites divisions, while Europe runs MX1, MX2, and MX3 classes.

James Stewart gets the "holeshot" and is first around the first turn in this motocross race.

Supercross

Supercross is similar to motocross, but the events are held on shorter, man-made tracks that are built in large stadiums. Up to 700 tons of dirt have to be trucked in to create these courses! These man-made monsters feature a mix of awesome tabletop jumps, rolling bumps known as **whoops**, and tight turns called **berms**. Supercross races usually have only 20 racers riding at the same time. In the U.S., races are divided into Supercross and Supercross Lites classes, depending on the size of the motorcycles.

The stadium version of the sport takes place in places normally reserved for baseball or football.

Arenacross

Arenacross competitions are much like supercross, but they are held in smaller arenas instead of massive stadiums. This means the that tracks are even smaller, with shorter straightaways and tighter turns. The jumps, however, can be just as big, and races are known for their big crashes. In the U.S., races are divided into Arenacross and Arenacross Lites classes.

Supermoto

Supermoto is a pulse-quickening combination of street racing and motocross. About 70 percent of the race is on a paved track, while the rest covers an off-road section that's covered in bumps and jumps. In the U.S., races are divided into Supermoto and Supermoto Lites classes.

Brave and daring Lance Coury shows off the gymnastic skills that are needed to perform in freestyle motocross events.

Freestyle

Freestyle, or FMX, focuses on the most thrilling part of motocross—the jumps! Riders accelerate quickly and then fly off huge ramps to do tricks (known as aerials) while soaring through the air. Judges rate each trick based on difficulty, **execution**, and creativity, and the rider who gets the most points from the judges wins.

Only the most versatile and talented riders can tackle the challenges of supermoto, a mix of street and dirt riding.

The Man

Often called the father of modern motocross, Belgium's Roger DeCoster—known simply as "The Man"—has played a major role in making motocross the powerhouse that it is today, both as a champion rider and as an always smiling ambassador **for the sport.**

A Superstar's Start

DeCoster was born in Belgium in 1944. Unlike many of today's motocross stars, DeCoster didn't start riding motorcycles as a child. Though he loved dirt bikes, he grew up the oldest in a large family that simply couldn't afford to buy one. As soon as DeCoster was old enough, he got a job in a motorcycle shop, working six days a week while still going to school to save up money. He got his first race bike at age 17, and it wasn't long before DeCoster's natural talents took over. In 1964, at 19, DeCoster won his country's junior 500cc motocross title—an impressive feat in motocross-mad Belgium.

Riding bikes slightly larger than today's models, DeCoster won dozens of titles in Europe.

DeCoster (left) now enjoys meeting and watching stars like Ricky Carmichael (right).

A Global Champion

One reason for DeCoster's success was that he was always willing to put in the hours of work that are needed to be a champion, allowing him to stay strong on his bike long after other racers had begun to tire. He earned his first Grand Prix victory in 1968, and over the next dozen years, he won a record 35 more 500cc Grand Prix races, including a stunning five world titles. Throughout this time, DeCoster gave himself another challenge: bring the excitement of motocross to America. In the early 1970s, American riders were way off the pace of the top European stars. DeCoster traveled to America to compete in the Trans-AMA Championship, which pitted the best American riders against the top Europeans. He won the event four years in a row (1974–1977). Thanks in part to DeCoster's impressive riding skills, Americans began to appreciate the amazing things that could be done on a dirt bike, changing the course of the sport in the U.S.

Coach DeCoster

DeCoster left riding the way he came in: a winner. He retired immediately after winning a Grand Prix race at the end of the 1980 season. DeCoster didn't give himself much time to rest. The week after hanging up his helmet, he flew to the United States to begin a new career managing and coaching young American riders. For proof of DeCoster's coaching skills, look no further than the Motocross of Nations. As a rider, DeCoster helped Belgium win the event six times. Once he started coaching Team U.S.A., the Americans went on to win a record 13 straight times! Inducted into the Motorsports Hall of Fame in 1994, "The Man" continues to play a vital role in motocross to this day. His appearances at MX events around the world still draw crowds. He also works with young riders to help them succeed.

It's Showtime!

Jeremy McGrath was the first American rider to become a full-blown motocross superstar. McGrath has appeared in video games, movies, and TV shows; his autobiography was a best seller! Thanks to all of this, McGrath's racing pals gave him one of the sport's coolest nicknames: Showtime!

McGrath moved from bagging groceries in high school to bagging trophies in MX!

The California Kid

Born in San Francisco in 1971, McGrath began his two-wheel career as a competitive BMX (bicycle motocross) racer. His heart, though, was set on the buzz of motorbikes, and he begged his parents to let him race motocross. They agreed, but only if McGrath helped pay for the costs. After saving money by bagging groceries, McGrath got his first motorcycle. In a few short years, the one-time grocery store clerk had become the "King of Motocross."

Supercross Superstar

Between 1993 and 2000, McGrath dominated the world of supercross, winning a total of seven out of eight 250cc AMA Supercross Championships. McGrath brought motocross racing to millions of new fans throughout his championship run, with crowds flocking to watch the **magnetic** star in action. McGrath also held his own racing outdoors in motocross, winning an AMA championship in 1995 and helping Team USA win the Motocross of Nations in 1993 and 1996. McGrath has "officially" retired from racing several times, but he keeps coming back for more. McGrath also races in the Championship Off Road Racing (CORR) truck series.

The Nac-Nac

Along with his other accomplishments, McGrath has played a key role in the rise of freestyle motocross. Supercross riders had long performed wild tricks off the final jump at the end of races, but McGrath blew crowds away during the 1994 season by busting out a trick that he borrowed from BMX called the **Nac-Nac**. While in midair, McGrath would swing one leg around the back of the bike and extend it outward as far as possible. Though relatively tame when compared to today's double backflips, the attention that McGrath's Nac-Nac received helped lead to the popular freestyle competitions held today.

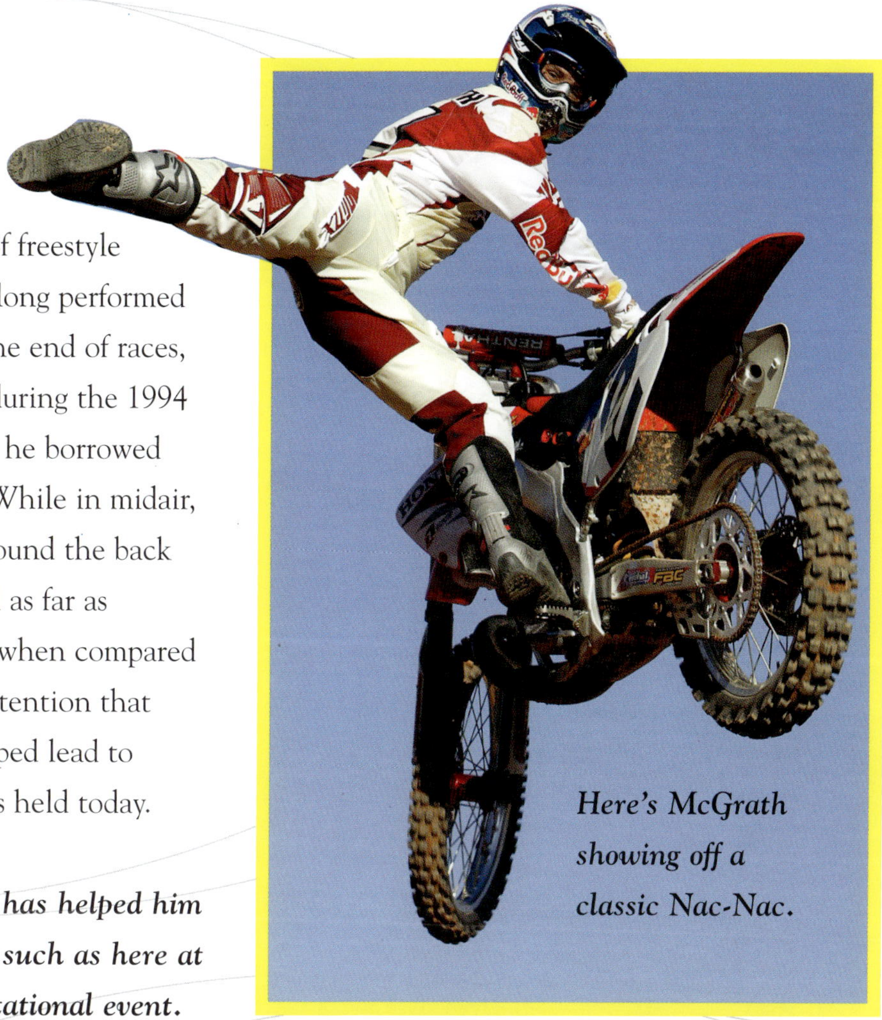

Here's McGrath showing off a classic Nac-Nac.

McGrath's success on the track has helped him promote the sport that he loves, such as here at the 2006 Jeremy McGrath Invitational event.

Stefan the Great

For thousands of motocross fans around the world, 72 is the luckiest number there is. That's because 72 is the number that's worn by Stefan Everts, the most dominating motocross rider in European history.

Belgium's Best

Though it's one of Europe's smaller countries, Belgium has always been one of the brightest lights in motocross. Belgian sports fans are **rabid** for the sport, and the list of champions born there—including Joël Robert, Eric Geboers, and Joël Smets—is nearly as long as a motocross track. Sitting side-by-side with Roger DeCoster at the top of the list is Everts, who retired in 2006 after winning a phenomenal 10 world championships. With 101 Grand Prix victories in total, Everts is one of the few riders to have earned the nickname "Mr. 875cc," having won world titles in the 125cc, 250cc, and 500cc motorcycle classes. (Why 875? Add up those other numbers, and see what you get!) In fact, Everts once managed to win all three classes on the same day in 2003, an incredible feat that motocross fans still marvel over. That versatility and ability to ride well on bikes of different sizes really set him apart from the rest of the motocross world. In his final season, Everts blew away the crowds at the Motocross of Nations in England by coming in first in both of his races—a great way to end his international career.

Portrait of a champ: Everts came from a small country to have a big impact on his sport.

The Boy from Bree

Born in Bree, Belgium, in 1972, Everts had a great coach standing nearby from his very first breath. His dad, Harry Everts, was a four-time motocross world champion himself, and he got Stefan to start racing before he turned five. Check out the *Guinness Book of World Records*—you'll see that both father and son are listed inside. Harry is tied for the world record of most 125cc world championships with three, while Stefan is tied for the world record for most 250cc world championships with seven.

"When you've got a dream, the more you fight for it, the bigger the chance you have to make it real. But you have to train hard and you've got to listen to what others have got to say. You also have to keep from believing you know everything best—because you learn most from your competitors."

—*Stefan Everts on what it takes to be a champion.*

Here's a good look at the heavy-duty protective boots that Everts and other riders wear.

G.O.A.T.

Motocross legend Ricky Carmichael didn't earn the nickname "G.O.A.T." by eating everything in his path. Instead, he earned it by beating everything in his path. His nickname stands for the "Greatest of All Time." Carmichael earned it with two decades of victories on tracks around the world.

Amid the churning dirt of an MX track, Carmichael (4) leads the way.

Zero to Hero

Born in Clearwater, Florida, on November 27, 1979, Carmichael began running laps on his family's dirt-bike track when he was only three. He started racing at the age of five, and soon enough, he was winning amateur events at a record pace. In 1996, Carmichael entered the professional ranks and was quickly named the AMA Motocross Rookie of the Year. It took only one more year for Carmichael to win his first championship, but the **brash** rider still had plenty to learn. Carmichael may now be one of the most beloved riders in motocross, but things weren't always that way. As a young pro, the overconfident Carmichael had to deal with booing fans after his wins. Willing to change his cocky ways, Carmichael worked on becoming nicer in victory. His **perseverance** and a positive attitude not only helped him win race after race—it also helped him win over the world of motocross.

Motocross Master

Total domination. Those two words sum up Carmichael's motocross career, and his list of records stacks as high as one of his tabletop jumps. Carmichael has the most wins in AMA competition, holds the record for the most AMA Motocross/Supercross Championships, and is the only rider who has never lost an outdoor championship. Most impressive, Carmichael has two perfect seasons under his belt, winning all 24 motos in the 250cc AMA Motocross Championships in both 2002 and 2004. No other rider has ever had even one perfect season. In his 11 years as a pro, Carmichael entered a total of 243 AMAs and won an incredible 150 of those. That means that Carmichael won just over three of every five pro races that he entered!

Along with speed and riding skills, Carmichael brought a great flair to his riding, such as this midair whip trick.

Following another supercross win, Ricky enjoys the cheers of the crowd.

The Final Countdown

All good things must come to an end, and the "Greatest of All Time" raced his final official moto on August 12, 2007. Not even a Hollywood movie writer could have written the day any better. The location was the Motocross of Nations at Budds Creek, Maryland. It was the first time in 20 years that the historic event had been held in the United States. In front of more than 50,000 flag-waving fans, Carmichael blasted off at the start of his final race and never looked back. Flying over the dirt track under sunny skies, the world's number-one rider came in first place, leading Team USA to its record 18th Motocross of Nations win.

A Fast Future

Carmichael is often called the "Michael Jordan of motocross." Just as Jordan is considered the greatest basketball player in history, Carmichael is the best motocross racer of all time. But their similarities don't end there. Just as Jordan took a break from basketball to play baseball when he was on top of his game, Carmichael decided to stop racing motocross to test himself with a new sport: **NASCAR**. Fulfilling a longtime dream, Carmichael announced in 2006 that he was switching over to racing cars.

A late 2007 **diagnosis** of a medical condition called chronic fatigue syndrome might slow Carmichael down, but as his fans from motocross know, it'll take a lot to keep this speed demon away from the track and from the competition. However, only time will tell if he can have the same success on the big oval track as he did on dirt.

"Ricky made a lot of guys wish he'd never been born or wish they had been born in a different decade. If Ricky had not come around, there'd be a lot more wealthier and famous riders out there."

Motocross champion Grant Langston (right) on Carmichael's dominating career.

It never got old, even though Carmichael enjoyed the thrill of victory hundreds of times.

King James

If you asked a room full of motocross experts which professional rider is most likely to take over Ricky Carmichael's throne, the answer you'd hear most would be James "Bubba" Stewart. Born in 1987, Stewart has been called the "Tiger Woods of motocross," after the great golfer who was a star while still young.

A Great Start

The similarities between Stewart and Tiger Woods go way beyond just their African American heritage. Both athletes are known for their positive personalities and ability to work hard. Both also perform at their best when the pressure is highest. And just like Woods, Stewart got into his sport at a young age. Stewart's dad, a former motocross rider himself, had young Bubba racing laps when the kid was only three! Stewart had his first **sponsor** at the age of seven, and by the time that his amateur career ended, Stewart had beaten even the great Ricky Carmichael's record for national wins with 11 (a mark that has since been broken by Kevin Walker with 13).

The Pro Show

Stewart began his pro career racing in the 125cc class (now known as the "Lites" class). Almost from the very first start, he dominated the competition. In 2002, he became the youngest 125cc champion in AMA history. Stewart won a total of four AMA 125cc Championships, and he still holds the record for combined supercross and motocross wins on a 125cc bike, with 47. In 2005, Stewart stepped up to the larger, more difficult 250cc class, and became the first African American to win a race in that class. A year later, he fought a dramatic race-by-race battle with Ricky Carmichael and Chad Reed

James Stewart was a fresh, young face who brought more attention to the sport with his hard work and great skills.

to earn his first World Supercross Grand Prix (GP) Championship. Stewart's crowning achievement took place in 2007, when he finally took home the AMA Supercross Series title.

"I'm happy to be in the position I am in and I hope that I can continue to help the sport grow from here... I will be working hard as ever because there will always be another fast guy coming up to challenge for the win."

James Stewart, after winning the 2007 AMA Supercross Series title.

This is the familiar green No. 7 motorcycle that Stewart has raced to successes including the 2007 AMA Supercross Championship.

Stewart (7) heads off an outdoor jump next to the great Ricky Carmichael.

The Globetrotters

Known as the Olympics of Motocross, the Motocross of Nations has been bringing riders and fans together from across the world since 1947. But that's just one of many events featuring an international crew of motocross maniacs. Meet some of the sport's top international champions.

Grant Langston

When South African Grant Langston was only nine, he had to get special permission to ride with adults. Riders his age were no longer any competition! By the age of 14, he was the youngest rider in South Africa to win a 125cc Senior National Championship. After that, he began circling the globe, racing everywhere from Belgium to Brazil. Now based in the United States, Langston continues to race against the world's finest. The 2007 AMA Motocross Championship and title are among his many career highlights.

South Africa's Grant Langston has made America his second—and winning—home.

A real "Italian stallion," Cairoli has become one of Europe's top MX racers.

Antonio Cairoli

Born on the island of Sicily, Antonio "Tony" Cairoli is set to be a star of European motocross racing for a long time. In only his second season in the Grand Prix, Tony became the youngest Italian ever to win a World Championship in 2005. In 2006, the high flyer wowed the crowd at the Motocross of Nations by winning the MX2+MX Open heat. In 2007, Cairoli won his second Motocross MX2 world title.

Chad Reed

The wonder from "**down under**," Australian Chad Reed blasted onto the motocross scene in 2001 by starring as an unknown rider and ending up with an impressive second-place finish in the 250cc World Grand Prix standings. After moving to the U.S. the following season, Reed continued his successful ways, winning the 125cc East Championship in 2002 and AMA Supercross Championship in 2004.

Australian Chad Reed heads into the 2008 season as one of the fans' favorites.

Country	Motocross of Nations Wins as of 2007
U.S.A.	18
Great Britain	16
Belgium	14
Sweden	7
Italy	2
Russia	2
Czechoslovakia	1
France	1

France's Sebastien Tortelli hopes to one day help his country add to their single Motocross des Nations title.

The Triple Threat

Considered the greatest freestyle motocross rider of all time, Travis Pastrana started riding dirt bikes when he was only four years old. Born in 1983, Pastrana was a world freestyle champ by the time he was 14. While most riders just pick one type of racing, Pastrana has won at freestyle and motocross . . . plus, he drives rally cars!

Wheel Champion

You'd need a giant truck to cart away all of the medals and trophies that the master of freestyle motocross has won by boldly soaring through the air. Pastrana has come in first at virtually every freestyle competition possible, including a record seven gold medals at the X Games. But he isn't just a jumper; Pastrana got his start racing motocross, and as an amateur he won an impressive five Loretta Lynn's National Championships. After turning pro in 2000, Pastrana kept up his winning ways by quickly winning the 2000 AMA 125cc National championship and the 2001 125cc East Coast Supercross Championship. A long list of painful injuries slowed down Pastrana's winning ways in motocross, but so did something else: boredom. Looking for a new challenge, Pastrana began racing rally cars in 2003. A "wheel" genius, Pastrana quickly raced his way to the top of that sport as well.

Pastrana made his first mark on motor sports by winning several motocross pro and amateur championships.

Thrill Seeker

For most of us, riding a roller coaster at the local amusement park fills our need for high-speed thrills. But for a daredevil like Pastrana, a roller-coaster ride would be time for a nap. The creator

of a long list of freestyle tricks, Pastrana is best known for his revolutionary double backflip at the 2006 X Games. Replayed over and over around the world, the run is the most famous moment in freestyle motocross. But if you thought that Pastrana might have retired from his daredevil ways after that, think again. In one recent stunt, Pastrana backflipped a motorcycle into the Grand Canyon and parachuted down. But Pastrana pulled off his craziest stunt yet in 2007 when he jumped out of an airplane without a parachute, relying on three friends with parachutes to catch him in midair!

Pastrana was the first to do a double backflip in a motocross freestyle competition.

Ouch! Pastrana, crashing below, shows off the down side of daring: bruises!

The Freestyle Fellowship

At events such as the X Games, FMX has become as popular as skateboarding, with thousands of screaming fans cheering on their favorite riders. Like Superman on a motorcycle, these three freestyle riders fly faster than speeding bullets and can leap—and flip over—tall buildings in a single bound! Let's meet some of the best.

Mike Metzger

One of Mike Metzger's earliest memories is of jumping his plastic Big Wheel off of ramps that his dad helped him build—when he was only three! "That's what I've done to entertain myself as long as I can remember—hit jumps," says Metzger. "When I first started riding a [motorcycle] as a kid out in the desert, the first thing my grandpa had me doing was hitting jumps." Known as "The Godfather" of FMX, Metzger helped pioneer the sport in the 1990s. Always ready to test out a new trick or jump, Metzger was the first rider to complete back-to-back flips in competition at the X Games in 2002. The feat earned him several medals, as well as the Athlete of the Games honor. But when you've earned a nickname as cool as The Godfather, you have to keep backing it up by proving that you're still one of the best. That's exactly what Metzger did by completing one of the most exhilarating freestyle tricks ever in 2006. Known as the "Impossible Jump," Metzger set a world record for the longest backflip on a motorcycle by jumping over the fountains in front of Caesar's Palace in Las Vegas on live TV.

"When I first started doing backflips, I couldn't believe it was me. Every time I looked at the TV and saw myself doing a backflip, it didn't seem like it was real. It looks a lot different than how it feels doing it!"

—Mike Metzger

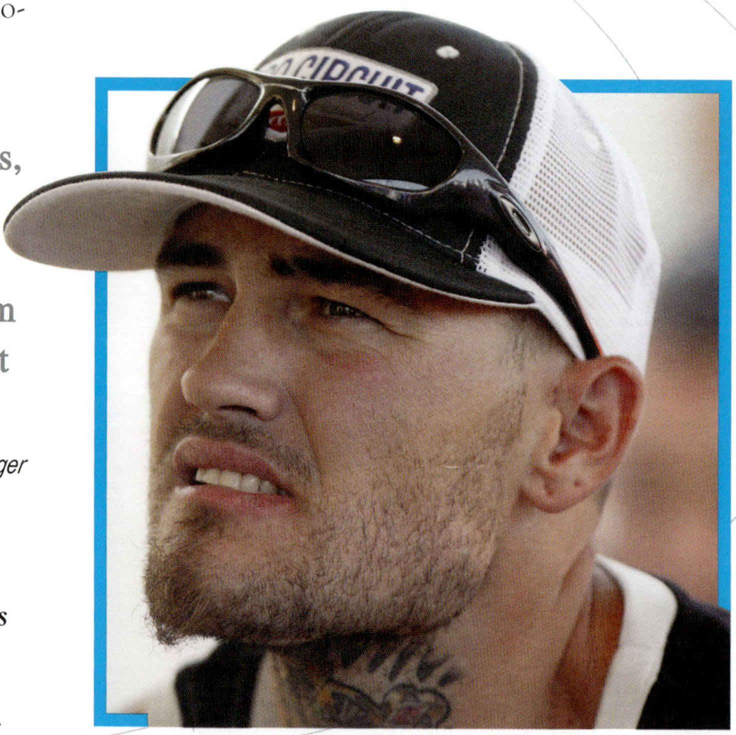

Mike Metzger is still pushing the boundaries of what freestyle MX riders can do, finding new and challenging ways to fly on his bike.

Nate Adams

If you want to rise up through the ranks of FMX, you can't just have one or two moves. You need a bag full of awesome tricks to keep judges and fans happy. That's the not-so-secret to Nate Adams's success: whether it's a 360 Nac-Nac or a "cordova backflip," Adams nails down a wide range of tricks with his smooth style. For proof of his impressive skills, look no further than his trophy case, which includes gold medals from the X Games and Gravity Games along with the AST Dew Tour's 2007 FMX Championship trophy. Even though he's earned the nickname "The Destroyer" for the way that he demolishes both tricks and the competition, Adams is actually a mellow fellow. He's far from flashy, and you won't find him strutting and screaming in front of the TV cameras at the next big competition. Instead, you'll probably find him standing on the podium accepting another medal. Adams knows that he doesn't need to brag, because his freestyle skills speak loud enough.

Adam Jones

A high-flying FMX competitor since 2002, Adam Jones proves that patience and hard work are a winning combination. For years, Jones would place high up in one competition, only to find himself lagging far behind in the next. But instead of giving up, Jones doubled up on his efforts, knowing deep down that one day his skills would shine through. And shine is exactly what Jones did in 2007, his big breakout season. Throughout the year, Jones placed in the top three in nearly every competition that he entered, including winning his first gold medal at the X Games in Moto X freestyle. How good was Jones' week? He won a silver medal for Best Trick at the same X Games, but only after entering as an alternate for an injured rider. Jones ended the year with a nasty crash that broke seven of his ribs, but he was still healthy enough to accept *Transworld Motocross'* prestigious FMX Rider of the Year award with a smile.

"Sure, I have low confidence, but I actually look at it as a blessing: My low self-confidence makes me work that much harder to prepare, and makes me try that much harder to compete."

—*Adam Jones,* Transworld Motocross

The laid-back Nate Adams laid out in style to perform this trick at the X Games.

Wonder Women

These days, seeing a woman zip around a motocross track at high speeds is no big deal. But it wasn't always that way. Back in 1971, Kerry Kleid had to hide her identity and pretend that she was a man in order to race. She later became the first female pro AMA rider. Meet some other stars who prove that motocross is far from just a man's world.

Good neighbors make good racers: here's Jessica (1) heading to the lead.

Jessica Patterson

If you're going to practice racing motocross, you can't do much better than having Ricky Carmichael around as a training partner. That's exactly what superstar Jessica Patterson had growing up in Tallahassee, Florida, where her dad and Ricky's dad were friends. Since the age of seven, Patterson grew up practicing and racing alongside some of the top male riders in the world. Some of Ricky's magic must have rubbed off, as in 2007, Patterson won her fifth WMA championship.

"Ever since I started, I have always raced with the boys… I still think today racing with the guys helps your speed and to be more aggressive on the track and so I carry that over to the women's class. I think that is what has gotten me to where I am today."

—*Jessica Patterson,* Florida Motocross Magazine

Tarah Gieger

When racer Tarah Gieger was a young girl, her parents bought her a motorbike instead of the go-cart that she really wanted. Instead of pouting, Gieger got on the bike and roared into a career as a professional motocross champion. Gieger's known for her hard-charging style of riding, and she has the injuries to prove it—including a broken collarbone, chipped **vertebrae**, and crushed wrists. She hasn't let crashes slow her down, and while she's won a WMA title and Lorreta Lynn National Championship, Gieger's proudest day came in 2007. That's when she became the first female in history to race in the Motocross of Nations, riding for Team Puerto Rico.

Sure, Tarah is smiling now—that's because she's between crashes!

Ashley Fiolek

Motocross maniac Ashley Fiolek hasn't let life's obstacles slow her down—instead, she's hopped on her bike and simply jumped over them. Deaf since birth, Fiolek has been riding and racing motorbikes since the age of seven. Though still a teenager, she's already earned a lifetime's worth of first-place trophies and awards, including being named 2004's AMA youth rider of the year. Now that she's competing in the Women's Pro ranks, Fiolek has become the first deaf professional motocross rider in history. But this ripping rider's dreams don't end with the women's circuit. Her ultimate goal is to become the first girl to qualify for a men's pro national. Considering how far Fiolek's come already, you'd be crazy to bet against her.

Bravery comes in many forms—Fiolek has not let her disability stop her from succeeding.

Villopoto Action

Every fresh-faced racer that hops onto a dirt bike has a dream of becoming the "next Ricky Carmichael." One rider who has the skills to reach that rare height is Ryan Villopoto, the newest and youngest superstar in motocross.

Flying Ryan

The idea that Villopoto could one day become as legendary a racer as Carmichael has nothing to do with the fact that they're both redheads or that they'd both rather let their riding do the talking than sit around blabbing about how great they are. Instead, it comes down to a quality that's hard to measure but easy to see—determination. Like Carmichael, Villopoto refuses to take a race lightly, and if a few riders need to be bumped aside along the way to the finish line, then so be it. Villopoto's stubborn streak has earned him some enemies, but it's also already won him a lifetime's worth of first-place trophies.

Dirty but happy: Villopoto's gear can't cover every inch of his face, so a little of the track ended up on his face . . . but he ended up in first place!

A Year to Remember

Born in Poulsbo, Washington, on August 13, 1988, young Villopoto can already boast about being a two-time MX Lites National Champion. He's the first rider since Carmichael to successfully defend his 125cc AMA National Championship, and he did it before even turning 20 years old. Villopoto's best year yet was 2007, when he was named motocross rider of the year by the sport's top magazines. His incredible performance at the 2007 Motocross of Nations helped cement the honor. At the race, he became the first rider ever to win both of his motos and the overall